David Milne-Home

Biographical Memoranda

of the persons whose portraits hang in the dining-room at Milne-Graden,

Berwickshire

David Milne-Home

Biographical Memoranda
of the persons whose portraits hang in the dining-room at Milne-Graden,
Berwickshire

ISBN/EAN: 9783337381943

Printed in Europe, USA, Canada, Australia, Japan

Cover: Foto ©Andreas Hilbeck / pixelio.de

More available books at **www.hansebooks.com**

BIOGRAPHICAL MEMORANDA

OF THE

𝕻ersons whose 𝕻ortraits

HANG IN THE

DINING-ROOM AT MILNE-GRADEN

(BERWICKSHIRE).

DRAWN UP BY

DAVID MILNE HOME, ESQ.

OF WEDDERBURN.

EDINBURGH:

PRINTED BY R. WALLACE & CO., HANOVER STREET.

———

MDCCCLXII.

Biographical Memoranda.

Pictures on West Wall.

I. Full-sized Portrait of SIR JOHN HOME OF RENTON, seated in a chair, and in his robes as Lord Justice-Clerk.

He was the first Clerk of the Justiciary Court who obtained a seat on the Bench. His commission as Judge is dated 1st December 1663. He had previously held a commission, dated 4th June 1663, as " Clerk and Maister of Ceremonies," in virtue of which last office, he had to attend " at the creation of all Earles, Lords, and Baronnes, and at all other solemn assemblies."—(Baron Hume's Commentaries, ii., p. 17.)

His grandfather, Patrick, was the second son of Sir Alexander Home of Manderstone. He had acquired the estate of Renton by marrying, in 1558, Janet Ellam, the heiress of Renton—or Raynton, as it was then called.

His father, Alexander, was Sheriff of Berwickshire from 1616 to 1621. He was zealous in the discharge of his functions; for it is recorded of him, in a letter from his son to Sir Patrick Home of Polworth (preserved at Marchmont), that he burnt several unfortunate persons as witches at Coldingham, in which parish he resided.

The following is an extract from this letter :—" I am veri " sorri it was not my fortune to know when y^r lo'p came to " Coldinghame, that I might have waited upon you, and " acquainted you with the great increase of witchcraft w^h

" is in that place. The slackness of judges for a long tyme
" has been the occasion; for there ware never any appre-
" hended there since my father was sheriffe, at wʰ tyme he
" caused burn seven or eight of them in that place. I know
" yʳ lo'p is inclined to doe justice, and it is only proper for
" yʳ lo'p to take notice of it. If some were apprehended,
" more would come to light. If yʳ lo'p desire to have a list
" of names, let me know, who is in all sincerity yʳ lo'p most
" affection. cousin and obed. servant,   A. HOME."

Sir John Home, the Lord Justice-Clerk, married Mar-
garet, eldest daughter of John Stuart, Commendator of
Coldingham Priory, and son of the Earl of Bothwell. By
her he had three sons,—viz., (1) Sir Alexander Home of
Renton; (2) Sir Patrick Home of Lumsdain; (3) Henry
Home of Kaims.

It appears that Sir Alexander was a person of somewhat
weak mind, and, at all events, ill fitted for business, of which
circumstance his father seemed to be aware. For Sir John
Home of Renton, in his settlements, whilst he left the estate
of Renton to him, as eldest son, gave to his second son Patrick
certain powers over that estate, for the management of it.
The consequence was that quarrels soon sprung up between
the brothers, and litigation went on between them, which
continued for more than twenty years, and of which the
reports of decisions in the law courts contain many records.
From these records it appears, that Sir Alexander, for some
time before his death, did not reside in family with his wife
and son.

It is supposed from this circumstance, and from the
minutes of the kirk-session of the parish of Coldinghame,
that Sir Alexander led a somewhat irregular life. A few
notices from these session records may be given, to show
the surveillance exercised in these days by the Church over
persons in all classes of society.

In the year 1696, it is noted that Mr Dysert, the minister of the parish, had gone to Sir Alexander, " and did deal with " him to extend his charity to the poor, especially to those on " his own ground ; and did exhort him, y^t seeing he comes " not out to church, y^t he would send his offering to the poor, " and y^t ye s^d *Sir Alexander* did promise to send his offering, " and to send some victual to those y^t were named to him " in his ground. And now information is made y^t he hath " sent some victual to one, and his offering to oyr box y^s day."

1697, *July* 4.—The first admonition to one (Sir Alexander Home of Renton—*suppresso nomine*) last Lord's day.

" He was advertised from the pulpit y$_s$ day that the p^{brie} " is to sit at Dunss on Tuesday the 6th inst., and certified y^t " if he do not submitt to the judicatory, and purge himself " by oath or take with the guilt of the crime laid to his " charge, the p^{brie} will proceed to the sentence. The con- " gregation was again exhorted to pray for this man, y^t " repentence unto life may be given unto him."

" 1697, *Sept.* 12.—This day was the second admonition " given out of the pulpit to *Sir Alexander Home of Renton,* " *expresso nomine,* in order to excommunication."

" 1698, *June* 12.—Given for the velvet cloth for *Sir Alex-* " *ander Home of Renton,* £3."

It would appear from the entries in these session records, that, prior to October 1699, Sir Alexander had died ;* for, of that date, notice is taken of Lady Renton, as in the management of the estate of Renton. He was succeeded by a son, Robert, who, from some subsequent notices, must then have been about seventeen years old.

In July 1701, a meeting of kirk-session was held, at which measures were spoken of for erecting a Bridge across the River Ale, situated on the Renton estate. The minutes bear that the minister reported " he had not yet spoken with

* Sir Alexander died 27th May 1698 (see Memoranda, page 5).

" *Sir Robert;* but he intended to do so next week, or at
" farthest when his mother comes home, considering his
" minority."   .

These kirk-session records contain abundant evidence
that *Sir Robert Home of Renton* must have been a scape-
grace.

" 1702, *April 5.*—James Megget rebuked for eating upon
" a wager.   He was interrogat whether or not, as is reported,
" he was guilty of eating upon a wager, to the scandal and
" offence of the place he lives in.—*Ans.* That he doth ac-
" knowledge that, lately being in company with *Sir Robert*
" *Home, and Mr Laurie his pedagogue,* there was some
" discourse of eating of eggs, and he did offer to eat a
" dozen, yea two, nay even three, if they would provide
" them, and that is all the wager talked oft ; and that he
" did eat the three dozen, as he said he would do ; and he
" did not know that this would be an offence, as it seems
" it is.   He was gravely rebuked for such discourse, and
" for boasting of his ability of eating much, and for making
" such an offensive experiment thereof.   And the report be-
" ing also flagrant, that after the said three dozen (eggs)
" were eaten, he offered to eat as many presently, and,
" within some little time, a considerable quantity of
" butter,—to this he did first answer, that it was but a
" story ; but when it was urged it would be found a true
" one, he next answered, that it was only said in jest.   He
" was further admonished and sharply rebuked for such
" idle, scandalous, and offensive discourse and jesting, that
" is not convenient, and cautioned for the future to take
" heed to his talk, for his teeth were like to shame him.
" He pleaded that what was done was done ignorantly, and
" craved pardon for the offence, promising that he should
" so carry for the time to come, that none should have
" reason to complain of him of such talk and jesting."

A more serious offence is referred to in the following
extract:—

"1702, *Nov.* 8.—Mr Dysert, minister of Coldingham,
" reported that (as appointed by the session) he did go to
" Renton, and did meet the lady aforesaid, and did desire to
" have Sir Robert spoken with. She said that he was some
" way out of the house, and that it was not so fitt here ; he
" would come to the manss, and speak with me there. How-
" ever, she declared that he denies all, is enraged at the
" report, and becaus she seemed to frown upon him, he
" threatened to go off the kingdom, with which she is much
" concerned ; and is also enraged at the woman her late
" servant, her parents and relations, and threatens to putt
" them all out of Renton ground, and is highly offended
" with William Hagues, brother-in-law to the said Nicholas
" English, whom she supposes to be the delator, and who,
" upon the said supposition, was beaten by Sir Robert,
" Monday last, and it seems with her approbation ;—which
" rage and outrageous carriage, as it is not to be liked, so he
" had evidenced his dissatisfaction with it, and displeasure
" against it, and exhorted the said lady to endeavour calm-
" ness, and deal with her son to confess and submitt, if
" guilty. In fine, the said lady desired that the business
" might sist, and so much the more, as the greater part of
" the family were going to Edenburgh for the winter."

"1703, *Oct.* 10.—The session, considering that *Sir Robert
" Home of Renton*, now at home, is too long forborn, after
" so much pains to gett him to come and answer for him-
" self, ... order was given to cite him. . . . . And as
" to Robert Hagues, Willm. Purves, elder, reporting that
" he had spoken to his mother anent him, and that she de-
" clared he was stubborn and would do nothing for her,
" and he being delated to the p^brie for contumacy, advice
" was given to pass and pronounce the sentence of the

" lesser excommunication against him, if he persist in re-
" fusing to satisfie discipline. It was recommended to the
" minister to commune with *Sir Patrick Home*, and to
" crave his assistance in regard that he (Hagues ?) dwells in
" a familie upon his ground, and to report his diligence
" next dyet."

" 1703, *Oct.* 17.—The minister reported his diligence in
" discoursing with *Sir Patrick Home*, and craving his assist-
" ance, and of Sir Patrick's concurrence in the affair, so
" effectually, that the said Robert Hagues did this day ap-
" pear publicly in the seat ordinary, and there, owning his
" said sin and scandal, was gravely rebuked for the same,
" together with his stubborn and contumacious carriage in
" their hearing, and recommended to the minister to return
" the session's thanks to *Sir Patrick Home*, and to desire
" his assistance to bring persons to obedience that dwell on
" his ground, and are lyable to Church censure."

" *Oct.* 24.—The minister reported his diligence in going to
" Renton and communing with *Sir Robert Home*, after some
" pains was used to gett access, and that he had promised to
" send this day a line as to his appearing before the session;
" and the line being sent accordingly, it was craving that
" the case be now forborn till the spring, at his return from
" Edinburgh. The session, considering the family, their
" principles, and the temper of the youth, besides his bash-
" fulness, referred his petition to the p^{brie} for advice, and
" they are to sitt upon Tuesday next."

" 1703, *Oct.* 31.—*Sir Robert Home*, his case being pro-
" pounded to the p^{brie} for advice, and his letter there read,
" after some communing upon that affair, the family being
" indeed engaged in a law-plea, and obliged to attend at
" Edinburgh, and *he now at age*, advice was given to delay,
" it being also then suggested that he intends to come out
" at Christmas, and wait upon the session."

" 1704, *April* 9.—The minister reported that he had gone
" to *Renton* and communed with *Sir Robert Home*, who,
" being to go to Edenburgh on Friday last, could not then
" condescend upon the time of his appearing to answer for
" himself, but had promised to acquaint Thos. Atcheson, the
" elder of that bounds, at his return, and who was appointed
" to attend him and report what he is resolved upon, and
" where he is to be mett with, his youthood and bashfulness
" being considered, and a session granted upon Renton
" ground for his answering to what is delated against him,
" if he conceive that an ease in the affair, though it was
" declared to him that it would be less noised if his appear-
" ing were at the ordinary place."

" 1705, *May* 6.—Thos. Atcheson, elder, his excuse for
" absence heard and sustained ; and an account being
" craved of his diligence in the affair committed to him,
" viz., of speaking to *Sir Robert Home*, and assisting the
" delator of the scandal above mentioned,—answer was
" made that he had discoursed with the delator anent the
" scandal ; and the offender being at some distance, he had
" not yet mett with him ; and that Sir Robert was so
" seldom in the countrey, and his stay short and uncertain
" when at home, that nothing was done as yet effectually."

" 1705, *May* 20.—Thos. Atcheson reported that he had
" mett with and spoken to *Sir Robert Home of Renton*, and
" had represented to him how inconvenient it was every
" way ; . . . . and that the said Sir Robert declared that
" he was obliged to be in Edenburgh this week about his
" affairs, *with his uncle Sir Patrick*, and could not con-
" descend to a day when he could attend the session."

" 1705, *Oct.* 21.—After conference anent the affair of
" Sir Robert Home, it was represented that the p[brie] had
" allowed the session to proceed according to the discipline
" of the Church with Nicolas Inglis, and that the case

" being efferred to, and considered by a considerable com-
" mittee of the synod, they also gave their opinion that she
" ought to be allowed as said is ; whereupon David Lock-
" art, elder, was appointed to speak to the said Nicolas
" Inglis, that she appear at the session next Lord's day,
" where order will be given for her public appearing. It
" was also represented that diligence has been used with
" Sir Robert and the Lady Renton for his answering for
" himself, and promise made by her to do what she could
" to persuade him, but as yet no answer."

" 1705, *Oct.* 28.—David Lockart, elder afforsaid, re-
" ported his diligence as to Nicolas Inglis, and withal that
" she was attending to know the session's order anent her ;
" and the min^r representing that he had again and again
" gone to Renton to see what Sir Robert Home would do
" as to that affair, and the Lady engaging to send him
" word, he being so very bashful, and she affraid that he
" go away, and word not being sent according to promise,
" he had again gone last week, and communed first with
" the Lady anent her diligence and success with her said
" sone, his answering for himself, and she signifying that
" he was utterly averse from any public appearing, and
" could not bring him to sett time and place for the session
" meeting with him,—desired that he be now spoken to at
" parting ; which being accordingly done, he had signified
" that within a few days he would meet with us, and that
" he would tell Thos. Atchieson, elder in the bounds ;
" which being considered, it was concluded that Nicolas
" Inglis, her appearing publicly, be forborn for a few days.
" The said Nicolas being called, compeared, her sin and
" scandal being spoken to, and again rebuked for the same,
" she expressed her desire to be allowed to satisffie Church
" discipline, to remove the scandal, and that she may be
" priveleged with scaling ordinances.   It was intimated to

" her that, within a few days, order would be given for her
" public appearing for these ends, and that David Lockart
" would acquaint her with it ;—and so dismist, with a
" serious exhortation to mourn before the Lord for the sin
" and scandal."

" 1705, *Dec.* 2.—The said day, did Nicolas Inglis appear
" in the seat ordinary for . . . . . , and was publicly re-
" buked for the sin of . . . . . , according to her confession
" before the session above recorded, with Sir Robert Home
" of Renton."

" 1705, *Dec.* 16.—The said day appeared Nicolas Inglis,
" for the second time."

" 1706, *Jan.* 13.—The said day did Nicolas Inglis
" appear for the third time before the congregation for
" the sin and scandal of . . . . . with Sir Robert Home
" of Renton, as is above confessed ; and the said sin being
" spoken to, and the said Nicolas having humbled herself
" upon her knees, and prayed, was dismissed in common
" form."

" 1708, *May* 9.—The session, taking to their serious
" consideration the diligence done in the affair of Sir
" Robert Home of Renton, both by session and p^{brie}, and
" the condescending terms offered by the session to him
" for his compearance before the session, and the too long
" delay in that affair, recommended to the min^r to write to
" him before any farther step be made, or any summons
" of awakening be given him for that scandal ; or, if health
" permitt, that he pay him a visit, and certifie him that the
" session will put the affair into the p$^{brie's}$ hands, if he do
" not answer for himself."

" 1708, *May* 30.—The minister represented that he had
" received a line from the moderator of the p^{brie}, signifying
" that he had written to *Sir Robert*, and expected his
" answer ; but the answer not coming, he advised that

" the said *Sir Robert* might be advertised by the session
" when he should attend them ; whereupon the session,
" taking to consideration the near approach of the Council
" and Session sitting down, and *Sir Robert's necessary*
" *attendance* there, they recommended to the minister to
" write to *Sir Robert*, and desire him to attend here on
" Thursday."

The volume of kirk-session records from which the
foregoing extracts have been made, does not extend to a
more recent date than May 1708, so that it is unknown
whether Sir Robert Home obeyed the summons of the
session to attend on the day specified. But enough of the
procedure has been detailed to indicate, both the low mo-
rality of the times, and the indiscreet zeal of the clergy in
attempting to correct it.

A farther illustration of ecclesiastical zeal will be found
in the following account of a frolic engaged in by John, the ·
son of Sir Patrick Home of Lumsden, and others equally
light-headed.

" 1704, *Oct.* 1.—A profane ramble committed this morn-
" ing, tabled, and delayed to ye next dyet."

" 1704, *Oct.* 5.—A scandal being related last dyet, the
" offence exceeding great, circumstances of time, place, per-
" sons, and actings considered, order was given to the elders
" in West-Reston to endeavour to gett the delinquents there
" to see the evil of such courses, and of being any wayes
" accessory to them ; and particularly to rebuke William
" Paxton, the piper, with certification of another sort of cen-
" sure if he do not mend his wayes ; and recommend to the
" minister to deal with the rest, either alone or with the
" assistance of other brethern, that they would consider the
" sin and folly of such childish, horrid, yea, hellish prac-
" tises, and to report ; and now, an account being craved,
" William Purves, elder in West-Reston, reported his

" diligence in the affair, and particularly in speaking to the
" piper aforesaid, who acknowledged his sin in going along
" with them, and promised never to do so again, and withal
" declared that he did attempt to gett from them, but he
" was constrained and threatened by *Alexander Home of*
" *Coldinghame-law,*—yea, that he did vow to stick him if
" he did not. The minister reported that he did go on
" Tuesday last, in company with Mr James Ramsay of Ey-
" mouth, to have spoken to *Mr John Home of Renton* and
" *Mark Ker of Houndwood,** but it was thought incon-
" venient then to crave access, they being a-bed, though it
" was near twelve o'clock. The session, considering the
" profane riot being committed in drunkenness on the Sab-
" bath morning when it was dark night, and having
" made enquiry, and getting intelligence that it was not in
" an alehouse, but elsewhere, that they were fudled, and
" that the persons are otherwise scandalous, it was farther
" recommended to the minister to deal with them, or with
" these that have authority over them, and to report."

" 1704, *Oct.* 22.—The session, considering further of the
" affair, recommended it to the minister to speak to *Sir*
" *Patrick Home* (he being here) ere *his son Mr John* were
" summoned, if he could not meet with himself, and with
" the other two also, if possible, Coldinghame-law being at
" Edenburgh."

" 1704, *Oct.* 29.—The minister reported, that having mett
" with *Mr John Home* and *Mark Ker* of Houndwood, he
" had discoursed with them. It was but a lame report that
" he could make, they alledging and insisting that the frolick
" was done on the Saturday, and so no such an offence as to
" be called before any ecclesiastical judicatory, and they were

---

* Dr Hood of Maines informs me, that Mark Ker is still traditionally
spoken of in the district of Houndwood and Renton, as noted for his dissipated life. He was called the " Knave of Clubs."

" sorry that so much ado should be made of it; and when it
" was efferred that, if need were, it could be proven that the
" riot was committed betwixt the hours of two and three on
" the Lord's day, it was replied that they were as tender of
" the Lord's day as others, and thought what they did was as
" said is. However, the thing being acknowledged by them,
" he had cautioned and admonished them for it, and certified
" them that, the same being so flagrant, the pᵇʳⁱᵉ had inter-
" posed their advice for citing them in common form, seeing
" they were not or could not be mett with. They pleaded that
" being now mett with, and the thing being discoursed, as
" above narrated, it was needless to make more ado about it.
" And *Sir Patrick Home* being spoken to anent the said riot,
" he acknowledged that he had heard something of it, and
" that *his son* had taken it ill that it was brought to public
" ere he was privately dealt with thereanent; but after some
" conference with him anent what was whispered, and the
" true matter of fact being efferred, both he and they saw
" that they were wrong informed. However, the said *Sir*
" *Patrick* conceived, that they being mett with, cautioned,
" and admonished, as said is, we should report the diligence,
" and make no more of it. As for *Alexander Home of Col-*
" *dinghame-law*, it was efferred for him, that having heard
" that the other two had been spoken to, he had promised
" to attend the minister on the Saturday ; but being at a
" race that day, he did not come."*

The parties implicated having refused to make either
apology or confession, the session proceeded to take evidence; and the first witness examined was " William Pax-
" ton (the piper), who asserted that it was sore against his
" will to come with them, but they constrained him, even

* I am indebted to Mr Andrew Wilson, merchant, Coldingham, for the
above extracts from the session records, as well as for much of the other
information given in these Memoranda.

" all the three, and would have him to ride behind one of
" them; which he refusing, Alexander Home gott on be-
" hind Mr John Home, and gave him his horse, and he
" conceives that it was but twixt the hours of 8 and 9 that
" they left Westreston, and terried in Cairn-corse-hall about
" an hour; and having mett with Whitfield at the end of
" his new dikes, they returned with him, and tarried in
" Whitfield about 2 hours, and that he loked his watch and
" it was about eleven a clock at night; and from thence
" they came straight to Lady Henderguest's, and having
" stayed there a little, they caused him to play, and a
" woman servant spake out at a window and reproved them;
" and then they came to the Manss (of Coldingham), and
" one of them came troue on horseback to the door, and
" that they caused him also to play then, but he asserted
" that he came not over the burn. It was told him that
" he was heard to be betwixt the house and brew-house,
" and that it was twixt the hours of 2 and 3 on the Lord's
" day. He acknowledged that, from the manss, they went
" back and returned through the town, and that still they
" caused him to play; that Houndwood and Mr John went
" to Alison Nisbet's* house, she being seen about the door,
" and what they said there he knew not; and that William
" Johnston, skipper, being at his door, in his shift, they
" caused come to them; and Thomas Watson being seen in

---

* Alison Nisbet was a reputed witch, to whom the following entry
in the Coldingham kirk-session records refer:—" 1698, *Oct.* 2.—Alison
" Nisbet being also cited and called, compeared. And being interrogat
" whither lately any had scratched or drawn blood of her above the
" breath ? *Ans.* Yes. Being asked who ? *Ans.* James Nicolson. Be-
" ing asked why did he bleed her ? *Ans.* Yt he called her witch, and
" then did bleed her. Being interrogat if any other had drawn blood
" of her? *Ans.* Tt James Fulton did throw a stone at her, and did
" hitt her upon the brow, and yt it was a mercy that he did not brain
" her."

" that habite, they urged to come with them; but he inter-
" ceding to get leave to put on his breeches, and winning
" to his house, bolted the door on them, and so they left
" him, but went to the Burnhall, where they danced and
" drank for some little time."

Another of the witnesses examined in this important investigation was the said Alison Nisbet. The minute of
12th November 1704 bears, " yt Alison afforsᵈ gave a satis-
" fying reason for her being up so soon on the Lord's-day
" morning, October the first, viz.,—the noise made then
" through the town by the above-mentioned ramblers with
" the piper afrighted her beasts, and made them break loose,
" and she was obliged to look after them lest they went on
" Bogangreen's grass, and so would be pounded; and withal
" asserted, that it was on the Lord's day that both Hound-
" wood and Mr John Home came to her house and asked
" her several foolish questions, and spake bad language; and
" that Houndwood offered to come in unto . . . and fashed
" her, till by the help of her son they gott the door shut."

After sundry other proceedings, the session, on 26th
November 1704, pronounced a deliverance in the following
terms :—" After some conference, the above mentioned and
" designed gentlemen being cited, and witnesses examined
" according to the advice of the pᵇʳⁱᵉ, and they proving con-
" tumacious, and the ramble proven, as said is, and extra-
" judiciallie confessed as above written, and judiciallie by
" the piper afforsaid, besides the declaration of Alison
" Nisbet and Thos. Watson, also above recorded, the pᵇʳⁱᵉ
" being to meet on Tuesday next, it was unanimouslye
" agreed to referre the said affair to the pᵇʳⁱᵉ for final de-
" termination."

What the determination of the presbytery was in the
affair, does not appear from these kirk-session records.

When the clergy in these days occupied themselves with

such trivial matters as are set forth in the preceding extracts, and made them the subject of solemn judicial investigation, it is manifest that they greatly mistook their true mission.

Nor need it excite surprise, if by such attempts at discipline they created a feeling in the community inimical to their authority, and unfriendly to the Presbyterian Church. Such seems to have been the effect in Coldingham ; for in these session records, under dates November and December 1708, the minister reports upon a " Schismatical Meeting " House" which had been set up, and " of the apostacy of " John and Katharine Fleming to Popery ; that they (the " pᵇʳⁱᵉ) might do therein according to the Acts of the " Assembly ; and represented that the synod, at their last " meeting, had recommended the affair of Schismatical " Meeting Houses to the pᵇʳⁱᵉˢ respective where they are ; " and that he had urged that ours might be carefully and " speedily minded by them."

On the 10th July 1709, it is noted that " The Sheriff " Principal has promised to suppress the Meeting House."

To resume the history of the Renton family, and trace their descendants, it may be explained that Sir John Home of Renton, the Lord Justice-Clerk, left the following representatives :—

1. *Sir Alexander Home of Renton*, the eldest son of the Lord Justice-Clerk, died 27th May 1698, and was succeeded by his only son, Robert, born about 1681. Sir Robert Home was succeeded, about the year 1752, by Sir John Home, whose name appears in the heritors' books as proprietor of Renton estate from 1667 to 1785. He died in 1788.

The estate was then inherited by Sir Alexander Stirling of Glorat, cousin of the said Sir John Home. He was the son of Miss Home, the sister of Sir Robert Home, who married a Mr Stirling in the year 1703. From the year

B

1793 to 1803, Sir John Stirling appears at the heritors' meetings as proprietor of Renton estate.

2. *Sir Patrick Home of Lumsdain,* the second son of the Lord Justice-Clerk, was created a Baronet in 1698. He was an advocate in Edinburgh, and seems to have been in very extensive practice. It is mentioned by Fountainhall, that he was the leading counsel for Robert Baillie of Jerviswoode, who was tried for treason in December 1684. Baillie was convicted, and hanged. He was accompanied to the scaffold by his sister-in-law, Lady Graden.

It is noticed by Fountainhall that, in March 1688, the Earl of Lauderdale, having to serve himself heir to his brother the Duke, he applied to Sir Patrick Home for some papers for instructing his brieve, which at first Sir Patrick refused to give, till compelled by an order from the Court of Session.

He was proprietor not only of Lumsden, but also of Alemill, Silverwells, Pilmuir, East and West Muirsides, Reston-mains, Reston-mill, Graystone-lees, and a good many houses in the town of Coldingham, including Burnhall, situated at the east end of the town. He appears to have rendered some important services—probably professional—to the Duchess of Lauderdale, for she disponed to him, as a recompence " for his services, the dwelling-house, " yards, orchards, and braes above and below the bridge " of Bruntstane." This was a small property situated between Portobello and Musselburgh. It remained in his family till sold by Sir John Home, as after mentioned.— (Fountainhall, vol. ii., p. 244.)

Sir Patrick Home had one son, John, and three daughters, Margaret, Elizabeth, and Isabel. He was succeeded by his son, Sir John Home, before referred to.

The tradition in the family is, that John was both dissipated and extravagant ; of which qualities the foregoing session records afford confirmation. In order to pay his debts, the estate of Reston was sold ; and Brunstane had also to be parted with under the following circumstances :— A whale having been cast ashore on his lands, Sir John claimed it as a " wreck," under his Crown Charter. The Crown, however, disputed the claim, and the case went ultimately to the House of Lords. Sir John lost his law-plea, and was found liable in expenses, which were so heavy that he had to sell Brunstane to pay them. There is a story, that, after selling this property, he refused to remove from it, and that when a messenger-at-arms was sent to expel him from the dwelling-house of Brunstane, he posted himself in a thorn tree, and swore that he would shoot ·the first man that ventured to come near the house. The thorn tree for a long time bore his name.

Sir John Home was succeeded by Sir James Home, his son, who sometimes got the title of Manderston, though belonging to a different proprietor, situated in the parish of Edrom.

Sir James Home is said to have been excessively benevolent and affable. He is even yet spoken of in the town of Coldingham as the " Good Sir James." One consequence of his benevolence and accessibility was, that he damaged immensely the interests of his family, by lending money to his friends, or becoming security for them. He was obliged to sell a considerable part of his lands to meet these obligations.

Sir James Home appears to have attended most regularly the heritors' meetings, probably from the circumstance of his residing at Burnhall. His name occurs in the minutes down to 1783. About the year 1752 he married Grace Johnston, daughter of Mr Johnston of Hilton and Hutton Hall, in the parish of Hutton.* It is known that he died in Decem-

* See Appendix (A) for an account of the other members of the Hilton family.

ber 1783, predeceased by his wife and an only son, and leaving two daughters, Margaret and Mary.

There is a person of advanced years now in the village of Coldingham (Mrs Paterson), who remembers Sir James Home's daughter. Her father and grandfather had been tenants of the family. As a girl, she was much taken notice of by the Burnhall Homes. She says that Margaret Home was "a handsome, noble-looking lady," and that Mary Home was considered "a great beauty."

Margaret never married. Mary, in the year 1775, married Sir Alexander Purves of Purves Hall. She was his second wife, and by him became the mother of the following children—James, Alexander, and John, Grace, Margaret, Mary, and Elizabeth. She died shortly after the birth of John. It is said, that she died of brain fever. Her sister was then on a visit to her at Purves Hall. Mrs Paterson relates, that on the morning following her arrival at Purves Hall, Mary came into her bed-room, in an excited state, dancing and singing, caused by the fever with which she had just been seized; shortly after which, she died. Margaret was so shocked and overpowered with grief, that she continued weeping night and day. Disease appeared in her eyes, and she became entirely blind. Her eyes eventually wasted away and disappeared. She died in the year 1796, aged forty-four. Although blind, she was able, not only to write letters, but to keep accounts. For writing, she had a small tablet, on which the paper was fixed, and over the paper a thin rod of metal was laid, kept firm at each end by a pin, in order to guide her hand in writing. When one line was written, this metal rod was moved down to the next row of holes, into which the pin dropped. Her accounts, she kept by means of a square table, perforated with holes in lines, into which she inserted pins. This table is now in my house, York Place, Edinburgh.

Margaret Home, shortly before her death, wished to sell Burnhall, and give or bequeath the proceeds to one of the Bairds of Newbyth, to whom she had been attached; but the transaction was not completed. On her death, the property went to Alexander Home Purves, the second son of her sister. His name occurs in the minutes of a meeting of heritors at Coldingham in the year 1796. He was an officer in the navy, and was drowned when at sea. He had not been married. The property then went to his younger brother, John Home Purves, who was an officer in the Scots Greys. When he succeeded, he was deeply involved in debt, which rendered it necessary for him to sell Burnhall and all the remaining lands belonging to the family. The price got was £17,000.

In the mansion-house of Burnhall, there were a number of old family pictures, which, shortly before the sale, were given in a present by John H. Purves to his elder sister Grace, then the wife of Captain, afterwards Admiral Sir David Milne.

These pictures were, with the consent of George Home of Paxton, brought by Mrs Milne to Paxton House, in order to be taken care of. They are referred to in the following directions by Mr Home to the trustees under his settlements :—

" *Paxton, 3d May* 1818.—The paintings in the house of
" Burnhall were given me by Mrs Milne, as most of them
" were the portraits of our common ancestors. She pro-
" bably would have kept them, if she had had a room at the
" time proper to place them in. Tho' I shall be better
" pleased they remain at Paxton, as the gift of an amiable
" and much respected friend,—if her son, David Milne,
" wishes to have them, I hereby authorise my trustees to
" deliver them to him."

(Signed)   " GEORGE HOME."

Mrs Paterson says, that on the death of Sir John Home, his son Sir James repaired and fitted up, for the reception of his mother, a large house in the town of Coldingham, which went by the name of The Castle. Sir James Home and his family occupied Burnhall House.

Mrs Paterson relates the following story. After Sir Alexander Purves married his fourth wife, Miss Hunter, and after the death of Margaret Home, the Purves Hall family used to reside at Burnhall for a few weeks every summer. On one occasion, immediately after their arrival, a fortune-teller entered the kitchen. Next evening, Mrs Paterson being at tea at Burnhall, the young ladies said to her, " Oh, Miss Young, (Mrs Paterson's unmarried " name,) what do you think sister Grace did yesterday ? " A spaewife came into the kitchen, and our Grace ran " down stairs to get her fortune told. And who do you " suppose is to marry her ? A brave sailor, a captain, " and the woman said the initials of his name would be " D. M. But as we know nobody whose name begins with " these letters, we wonder who it can be."

3. *Henry Home of Kaimes* was the third son of the Lord Justice-Clerk. He inherited from his father the lands of Northfield, in the parish of Coldingham, which are still in the possession of his descendant, Henry Home Drummond of Blair-Drummond.

Henry Home having died about the year 1692, was succeeded by his son George, whose son Henry, born 1696, became Lord Kames, distinguished as a lawyer, a historian, and an agriculturist. He became advocate in 1723, and a Lord of Session in 1752. He died the 27th December 1782. His name appears in the minutes of the heritors of Coldinghame during the years 1768, 1773, 1774, 1776, 1780.

He erected an obelisk on his grounds, at a spot where it

formed a conspicuous object, and he put on it this inscription :—

FOR HIS NEIGHBOURS,

AS WELL AS FOR HIMSELF,

THIS OBELISK WAS ERECTED

BY

HENRY HOME.

Graft Benevolence on Self-love,
The fruit will be delicious.

When asked by Sir J. Dalrymple how he was able to do his business as a judge, and write on so many other subjects, he replied, that " he took much time to do the " smallest thing; and that everything was to be done by " labour, and little by genius."

He married Agatha, the second daughter, and ultimately heiress, of James Drummond of Blair-Drummond, whose grandson Henry is now proprietor of Northfield. He is said to be the male representative of the Earldom of Dunbar, created in 1604. The present Mr H. H. Drummond's father was George Drummond Home.

II. Half-size Picture near top of wall, being portrait of a gentleman, in a full wig, and white lace neckcloth, and brown silk mantle.

This is believed to be the portrait of SIR ROBERT BAIRD OF SAUGHTON HALL, grandfather of Margaret Baird, the wife of Sir Patrick Home of Lumsdaine.

III. Half-size Picture, being portrait of a gentleman, in a full wig, white plain neckcloth, and lawyer's black gown.

This is believed to be the portrait of SIR PATRICK HOME OF LUMSDAINE, second son of the Lord Justice-Clerk before referred to.

He was married to Margaret Baird.

His eldest daughter, Margaret, was, in 1695, married to George Home of Wedderburn.

He is, in his daughter's marriage-contract, designed " advocate."

IV. Half-size Picture, being portrait of a lady, with high forehead, and bare neck, and loose dress.

This is believed to be the portrait of MARGARET BAIRD, wife of Sir Patrick Home of Lumsdaine.

V. Half-length Portrait of a gentleman, dressed in a coat of mail.

This is believed to be the portrait of SIR GEORGE HOME OF WEDDERBURN, who was attainted for taking part in the rebellion of 1715.

He was the son of Sir George Home of Wedderburn, by Isabel, daughter of Sir Francis Liddell of Ravensworth.

He married, in 1695, Margaret, daughter of Sir Patrick Home of Lumsdaine. The original contract of marriage is now in Paxton House. Among the witnesses to the contract are—Patrick Lord Polworth; Sir John Baird of Newbyth, one of the Senators of the College of Justice; Sir Robert Baird of Saughton Hall; William Morison of Prestongrange; Sir William Baird, younger of Newbyth; John Home, brother to the bride.

By the contract, George Home undertook to maintain his grandmother, Katherine Morison, the daughter of Lord Prestongrange.

George Home, with almost all the rest of the clan of Homes, espoused the cause of Prince Charles, and accompanied the rebel army into England. He was at the battle of Preston, where he was taken prisoner, and carried to the Tower of London.*

* In the records of the kirk-session of Coldingham, of the 20th No-

On being sentenced to be beheaded, he sent, as a farewell token to his wife, a small gold ring, with the device on it of a death's head, and his own initials. This ring is in the possession of Mrs Milne Home. It was given to her by the late Lady Milne.

Sir George Home was unexpectedly respited, and subsequently pardoned,—owing, as it is said, to an affidavit emitted by the minister of Dunse, that he was either above or below a certain age, though the affidavit was not in that respect strictly correct.

He returned to Wedderburn, where he is said to have died in the year 1717, leaving one son, David, and his widow.

His brother, Francis Home of Quixwood, advocate, had married Elizabeth, second daughter of Sir Patrick Home. He also being an adherent of the Stuart family, was transported to Virginia, where, in 1717, he became factor to the Governor. He died there in 1723. He left two sons, Alexander and John.

The estate of Wedderburn had previously been burdened to a large extent with debts, and, for payment of these, it was sold by the Crown. The principal creditor was a Mr Ninian Home of Billie,—which estate of Billie had been purchased by him some years previously, from the Rentons. This man was a person of extraordinary sagacity, and some special notice of him may not be uninteresting.

In July 1717, Ninian charged David Home to enter heir

---

vember 1715, there is the following entry:—" We had good ground this " day, and for ever, to bless our good God for the glorious victory ob- " tained by our King's forces, under the command of the Duke of Argyle, " near Dunblane, on the 13th inst., and that by a few, against many " rebels, under the command of the Earl of Mar ; and for a total rout, " at Preston, in Lancashire, the said day, of the Scots and Northumber- " land rebels, by our King's forces, under the command of Lieut.-General " Carpenter and Major-General Wills."

to his father, grandfather, great-grandfather, and great-great-grandfather, all of whom seem to have contracted debts, to which Ninian had acquired right.

On 18th February 1729, Ninian Home obtained from King George II. a charter, by which there were disponed to him the lands, barony, and estate of Wedderburn, in payment and satisfaction of the debts due to him.

Some few particulars of Ninian's family may here be given.

His father was Abraham Hoome of Rumbleton-law and Bellshill, in the parish of Home. His mother was Isabell Trotter, in the parish of Kelso. She is said to have been one of the Mortonhall family. Proclamation of the intended marriage was made in Gordon parish, 6th February 1670. The marriage was celebrated 1st April 1670, in the parish of Home and Stitchell.

Ninian was the eldest son of the marriage, and born 5th December 1670. He had a brother, James, and a sister, Mary.

He was, when a lad, clerk to James Daes of Cowden-knowes, advocate. Afterwards, he was educated for the Church, and first became parish schoolmaster at Fogo.* He was ordained minister of Buncle and Preston in 1696. In September 1700, he married Margaret Daes, daughter of the said James Daes. (The marriage-contract is among the Billie papers.)

In 1708, he was transferred to the parish of Sprouston, in the county of Roxburgh, from which he was deposed in 1718, for disaffection to Government.

By Margaret Daes he had two sons, Alexander and George, the former of whom became afterwards proprietor of Jardine Field, in the parish of Whitsom. Margaret Daes died in 1723.

* Appendix (B).

Until the year 1728, Ninian Home remained a widower. Even before his first wife's death, he had become intimate with the Wedderburn family. Perhaps the circumstance of his having lent large sums of money to the proprietor of Wedderburn, and of his having obtained bonds of annual-rent over the estate, occasioned frequent opportunities of intercourse. The Wedderburn title-deeds show that, in 1716, Ninian Home was infeft over Wedderburn in an annual-rent of £280 : 3 : 4. In 1717, another annual-rent of £590 : 6 : 10 was acquired by him over the lands of Wedderburn, Paxton, and Horndean.

Sir George Home of Wedderburn, at his death in 1717, left a widow, two sons, David and Patrick, and two daughters, Margaret and Jean.*

The family tradition is, that Ninian Home wished his son Alexander (by Miss Daes) to marry Margaret Home of Wedderburn. But Alexander had formed a preference for Jean, the younger sister, whom, accordingly, he married, much against his father's inclination. One consequence of this step was, that his father quarrelled with him, and that he left nothing to him by will. Another consequence was, that Ninian married the eldest daughter himself, in the year 1728, he being then fifty-eight years of age.

Ninian, by Margaret Home, had the following sons,— Ninian, Patrick, Abraham, David, Andrew, and Thomas; and three daughters, Isabel, Jean, and Margaret. These children were all alive in the year 1738, for they are named as substitutes of entail in the entail of Linthill, executed in that year by Ninian Home. There may have been other children, who had died before that date. There appear to have been Francis and John, alive in the year 1721.

Alexander, the son of Ninian, by Jean Home, had two sons, Ninian and George.

* Appendix (C).

In the Appendix (D) will be found three letters,—one from Lady Billie, Ninian's wife, and two letters from Ninian himself, dated 12th January 1721. I am unable to say who *Geordie* was, except that, from Lady Billie's letter, he appears to have been a son of old Ninian; and, therefore, the one he had by his first wife.

Ninian lived till 17th December 1744, by which time he had become proprietor of a large extent of lands. The Billie estate he had purchased about the year 1709, from the old family of Rentons. Wedderburn he acquired in the manner already explained. Linthill he obtained in the year 1737, by purchase from William Home, to whom he paid for it, £40,000 Scots.

He had acquired great influence in Berwickshire, from his own known sagacity, and from having lent large sums of money to its landed proprietors. The Billie charter-chest contains a bond for 16,000 merks over Lumsdaine, by Sir Patrick Home and his son, in the year 1718; likewise a bond, in the year 1720, over half of the lands and barony of Hirsel, belonging to the Earl of Home. From the correspondence extant, he seems to have exercised considerable political influence, as there are letters to him from Lord Milton (then Lord Justice-Clerk, the dispenser of Government patronage in Scotland), the Duke of Roxburghe, Earl of Home, Andrew Fletcher, &c.

It appears that, in the year 1733, Ninian executed an entail of the estate of Wedderburn, calling to the succession, not his own children in the first instance, but the sons of the attainted proprietor.

In 1738 he executed an entail of Linthill, calling to the succession of it, first the sons, and then the daughters, of his second wife; and after them, George, his second son by his first wife. Alexander, his eldest son by his first wife, who had offended him by marrying Jean Home, was excluded from all his settlements. It is a tradition in the family, that neither he nor his wife were ever allowed to come to Wedderburn, and that they lived in great penury.

Ninian was survived by his widow, Margaret, afterwards known by the name of Lady Billie, or Lady Branxton.

Her testament, dated 13th August 1751, is extant among the Billie papers, by which she appoints, as her executor, Abraham Home, her second son then in life. The deed is dated at Linthill, the house in which shortly thereafter she was murdered by her butler Norman Ross, when the rest of the family were absent on the occasion of a ball. Ross was tried and convicted. The following particulars are given in Baron Hume's Commentaries. It appears that before she died, Lady Billie declared before witnesses that Norman Ross " was the person who had done the bloody deed, and " directed them to look for the knife, which was accordingly " done, and found beneath the bed, besmeared with blood." Ross was hung in chains, his right hand being first cut off.

On the death of Ninian Home, the *Billie* estate, which belonged to himself, was inherited by his eldest son then alive, Patrick, of the second marriage, and the *Wedderburn* estate was inherited by David, the brother of his second wife, as heir of entail under the deed before referred to. On the death of David, in 1762, he was succeeded by his only surviving brother, Patrick, a surgeon in the navy, who died unmarried in 1766, and with him were exhausted the sons of George the Attainted.

The succession then opened, in terms of Ninian's entail of 1733, to his own children by his second wife, Lady Billie, —viz., Patrick Home of Billie, advocate,—and in him the estates of Wedderburn and Billie were combined.

Patrick Home was Member of Parliament for the county of Berwick. It was by him that the collection of paintings now at Paxton House was formed.

He lived till 1808, when he was succeeded by General David Home of Caldra, who died in 1809.

The General was succeeded by his only sister surviving, Jean, and she died in December 1812.

She was succeeded by George Home, the younger son of Alexander Home of Jardine Field. George Home and she were doubly related. He was full cousin to Jean Home, their mothers having been sisters. He was also nephew to her, as Jean was his father's half-sister.

How long Lady Wedderburn (the widow of George the Attainted) survived, is not known.

VI. Half-length Portrait of a lady, with a lock of hair over her left shoulder. Believed to be MARGARET HOME OF LUMSDAIN, the wife of Sir George Home, and who was ultimately known as LADY WEDDERBURN.

The frame of the picture corresponds in size and pattern with that of No. V.

VII. Full-length Portrait of GEORGE, EARL OF DUNBAR, and BARON HOME OF BERWICK.

He was the fourth son of Alexander Home of Manderston, by Jean, daughter of Home of Spott.

He is spoken of in a tack granted to him by his father and mother, dated 5th November 1585, and there designed " one of the Master Stablers to His Majesty King James VI." Prior to 1592 he was knighted, with the title of Sir George Home of Primrose Knowes.

In 1595, he received a charter of the barony of Greenlaw, in favour of himself and of Elizabeth Gordon, his spouse. In this deed he is designated Sir George Home of Spott.

In 1603, he was appointed Keeper of the Castle of St Andrews.

In 1604, he was created Earl of Dunbar, the title being devised to his heirs-male.

He accompanied James VI. to London, where he was appointed Chancellor of the Exchequer for England, and Lord High Treasurer for Scotland. He was made also Captain of the Guard formed to keep order in the Eastern Borders of England and Scotland.

Archbishop Spottiswoode says of the Earl of Dunbar, that he was " a man of deep wit, few words, and in His " Majesty's service no less faithful than fortunate. The " most difficult affairs he compassed without any noise, " and never returned when he was employed, without the " work performed, he was to do."

He was the person on whom King James most relied to bring about the restoration of Episcopacy in Scotland, which he managed so well, that he carried an Act to that effect through the Parliament at Perth in 1606. In that year, and in 1608, he was Lord High Commissioner to the General Assembly. The following notices from Scotch historians devoted to Presbytery, show the dislike entertained towards him by members of the Kirk.

Row, in his History, says,—" Sir George Hoome, now " Earle of Dumbar, came in great favour with the King, " and was so highly preferred that he was sent down to " Scotland and imployed in affaires of high concernment " both in kirk and countrey, and was honoured as a great " prince and ruler in this kingdome."

The Rev. John Forbes says,—" The Erle of Dumbar, " His Majesty's Grand Commissioner, and some of the " barons, met at Linlithgow, with the commissioners sent " from presbyteries, upon the 10th December 1606."

" The 69th Assemblie was keept at Linlithgow the last " Tuesday of Julie 1608, the Erle of Dumbar commis- " sioner."

Calderwood, in his History, records that, " upon the " Lord's day, 24th Aprile 1609, Dumbar made a solemne

" feast in the toun of Berwick. He was served as one of
" the Knights of the Garter by lords, knights, barons, and
" gentlemen of good ranke. A great number of people, both
" Scotish and English, were at that feast, which was made
" according to the English fashioun. Beside this feast, made
" in honour of St George the patron of England, he used
" certane ceremoneis in the kirk ; for he went to the kirk in
" pompe, where were standing upon the altar two chandlers,
" eache having a waxe candle burning, and a booke upon the
" altar. He bowed reverentlie upon the altar, in remem-
" brance of St George. Thereafter he made reverence to
" the king's picture placed beside, and then kneeled doun on
" his knee before the altar, where was a man standing beside
" with a silver basin, wherein he layed some peeces of gold.
" After this offering made, he heard a sermon, wherein was
" muche commendatioun of the King and of the Erle of
" Dumbar. After sermoun, he went to dinner, convoyed
" with lords, knights, barons, gentlemen, and souldiours."
The same historian relates that, in 1610, " The Erle of
" Dumbar was sent doun with commissioun from the King,
" and with him three English doctors (Hamptoun, Mirri-
" toun, and Hudsone). The Chanceller, and sindrie Erles,
" Lords, Barons, and gentlemen, to the number of sixteene
" hundreth hors or thereby, accompaneid the Erle at his
" entrie to Edinburgh upon the 24th May. The Proveist,
" Bailliffes, Counsell, and a number of burgesses, were
" attending in the utter closse of the palace to welcome
" him. That same day, after rysing of the Counsell, there
" were two silver maces or wands, overguilded with gold,
" caried by two gentlemen, the one before the Erle of
" Dumbar, the other before the Chanceller. This cere-
" monie was observed daylie after, wheresoever they went."
The same historian relates that, at a " meeting of the
" General Assemblie of the Kirk of Scotland, holden in

" Glasgow the 8th June 1610, the Erle of Dumbar ap-
" peared as Chief Commissioner, by the appointment of
" the King."

Row, in his History of the Kirk of Scotland, says,—
" When news came to England what was done at Glasgow,
" and Mr Andro Melvill, then being in the Tower, was in-
" formed of all the particulars, (James Colvin) a gentleman
" of his aequaintance came to take leave of him, and asked
" what word he had to send to his friends in Seotland. Mel-
" vill answered, I have no word to send to them ; but am
" heavilie greeved that the glorious government of the Kirk
" of Seotland should be so defaced, and a Popish, tyrannical
" government sett up : ' And thou, Manderstoun (so styling
" ' the Erle of Dumbar), hes thou no other thing to doe but
" ' to earie doun to Seotland such eommissions, whereby
" ' God's Kirk is wracked there ? The Lord shall be
" ' avenged ; and thou shall never go doune againe, for all
" ' thy grandeur.' He was busselie eompleating his great
" building in Berwiek, to have keeped St George's day there,
" and to have eelebrat, with great pompe, the marriage of
" his daughter with the Lord Waldoun."

The Earl of Dunbar had no sons. He had two daughters.
The eldest was married to Sir James Home of Cowden-
knowes. Her son became James Earl of Home. The
second daughter was married to Theophilus Howard, Lord
Walden, afterwards Earl of Suffolk. Her father was pre-
paring to eelebrate this marriage with great magnificence,
at his residence in Whitchall, when he was suddenly eut off,
on 29th January 1611, under the strong suspicion of having
been poisoned. Indeed, Sir John Scott of Seotstarvet ex-
pressly affirms that he " was poisoned with some tablets of
" sugar, given him for expelling cold, by Seeretary Ceeil ;
" whieh was well known by the death of one Martin Sougir,
" a doetor, who, by laying his finger on his heart, and touch-

C

" ing it with his tongue, died within a few days thereafter.
" The servant of his chamber, Sir James Baillie, saw him
" get the tablets from the said Secretary ; and who, having
" eaten a small parcel of them himself, struck all out in
" blisters, but by strength of body he escaped death." It is
alleged that, owing to the high appointments held by him,
and to the favour shown to him by the King, he had in-
curred the jealousy and hatred of the English courtiers.

Calderwood mentions that, in 1611, " The Chanceller, ac-
" companied with some other noblemen, tooke journey, the
" 11th Februare, to Berwicke, to take inventour of the Erle
" of Dumbar his moveables, as they had done before at
" Halyrudhous, conforme to the King's commission directed
" them thereanent."

There is an account, printed by the　　　　　　Club, of a
journey to Scotland made by Lord Walden in August 1614,
in the course of which he visited his brother-in-law, Sir
James Home, and his lady, then residing at Broxmouth, near
Dunbar, and the Earl of Home, then residing at Dunglass.

In the Billie charter-chest, there are two documents
which mention some of the lands belonging to the Earl of
Dunbar in Berwickshire.

(1.) One of these is a Crown charter, dated 4th April
1603, confirming, in favour of Sir George Home of Greenlaw, a charter by Sir Archibald Douglas of Pittendriech,
of the following lands :—

The lands of Samson's Walls and Crumstane.
The dominical lands of the Maynes of Dunse.
Seven husband-lands in the territory of Quhitsom.
Two husband-lands in the town of Hiltoun.
The lands of Prestoun.

(2.) The other document is a feu-contract, dated 1614,
granted by the Earl of Dunbar's two daughters, therein
designed as Lady Anna Hoome, spouse of Sir James

Hoome of Whyterig, and Lady Elizabeth Hoome, spouse
of Lord Theophilus Lord Walden. This contract included
the following lands:—

Flemington.

Twelve husband-lands of Netherbyres and Redhall.

Twelve husband-lands of Nether-Ayton.

Four husband-lands of Gunsgreen.

Sir John Scott states that his estates in Berwickshire
were divided between his daughters, and that they were
sold, viz., the lordship of Berwick to Sir James Douglas,
brother of the Earl of Angus, and the rest to the Earl of
Haddington.

A very handsome monument, in Italian marble, was
erected to his memory in Dunbar Church, which is said
to have been prepared at Rome. When the old church was
pulled down, it was removed to the new church, where it
now is, in good preservation. Some repairs on it were, it is
believed, executed by the Duke of Roxburghe, in the year
1820.

Pictures on East Wall.

VIII. Full-size Picture of the DUCHESS OF LAUDERDALE,
said to have been painted by Sir Peter Lely. This fact is
stated in an old catalogue at Paxton House, and used to be
mentioned by Lady Milne, as a tradition in the family.

In Walpole's Anecdotes of Paintings, there is a list of some
of Lely's paintings, and among them is a portrait of John
Maitland, Duke of Lauderdale, as at Ham House. This
circumstance adds to the probability that he painted also the
Duchess, the Duke's second wife, the Countess of Dysart,
who, besides being celebrated for her beauty and talent, was
very vain of both.

It is mentioned by Walpole, that Lely executed many
more portraits of women than of men; and he gives a de-

scription of his style of painting, which seems to suit the
painting in question. He says that Sir Peter's " portraits
" are generally to the knees. His laboured draperies flow
" with ease, and not a fold is placed but with propriety.
" Lely's dresses are a sort of fantastic night-gown, fastened
" with a single pin. He was, in truth, the ladies' painter;
" and whether the age improved in beauty or in flattery,
" Lely's women are certainly much handsomer than those
" of Vandyck. They please as much more, as they evi-
" dently meant to please. He caught the reigning character,
" and

" ———— on animated canvas stole
" The sleepy eye that spoke the melting soul."

A few extracts from the historians of these stirring times,
bearing on the character and doings of this extraordinary
woman, may not be uninteresting.

Mr R. Chalmers, in his Domestic Annals of Scotland
(vol. ii., p. 348), says, that " the Duke (of Lauderdale), at
" fifty-seven, and it is said only six weeks a widower, mar-
" ried the Duchess in February 1672, all their friends in
" Edinburgh making feasts on their marriage-day, while
" ' the Castle (of Edinburgh) shot as many guns as on His
" ' Majesty's birth-day.' Her Grace, now forty-five years
" of age, was, in her personal qualities and history, a most
" remarkable woman. Her wit and cleverness were some-
" thing singular; ' nor had the extraordinary beauty she
" ' possessed while she was young, ceded at the age at
" ' which she was then arrived.' The daughter of one who
" had been minister of Dysart, she was Countess of Dysart
" in her own right; and, by Sir Lionel Tollemache, had
" had a large family, which is still represented in the Peer-
" age. There was something romantic in her union with
" the now all-powerful Lauderdale. He had owed to her
" his life, through her influence with Cromwell; and in his

" marriage, which was disapproved of by all his friends,
" ' he really yielded to his gratitude.' For the next ten
" years, it might be said that Lauderdale and his clever
" Duchess, were all but nominally king and queen of Scot-
" land."

" On the Scottish Parliament meeting (12th June 1672),
" under the Duke as Commissioner, his ' lady, with the num-
" ' ber of thirty or forty more ladies, accompanies the Duke
" ' to the Parliament in coaches, and are set down in the
" ' Parliament House, and sat there to hear the Commis-
" ' sioner's speech,'—(Law)—' a practice so new and extra-
" ' ordinary, that it raised the indignation of the people
" ' very much against her, they hating to find that aspired
" ' to by her, which none of our queens had ever attempted.'
" It ' set them to inquire into her origin and faults, and to
" ' rail against the lowness of the one, and their suspicions
" ' of the other. . . . This malice grew daily against
" ' her.' "

Charles Kirkpatrick Sharpe of Hoddam, in his Memoirs
of Viscount Dundee and his Times, says that the Duke of
Lauderdale, in the severe measures he adopted against the
adherents of Presbytery, was much influenced by " his wife,
" a woman every way extraordinary and matchless.

" She was the daughter of William Murray, son of
" the needy minister of Dysart, and nephew of Charles
" I.'s pedagogue, who got his relative placed about his
" pupil in the station of page and *whipping-boy*, a crea-
" ture to be beaten whenever the prince was naughty,
" in order to scare him with the sight of punishment. As
" the king is said to have been a very froward child, young
" Murray would suffer in proportion; and it is to be pre-
" sumed that his flagellations obtained the gratitude of his
" master. First he was made a baronet, and at last he
" procured the patent of an earldom, and then married

" Elizabeth Bruce, of the Clackmannan family. By her he
" had two daughters, of whom the eldest, afterward Duchess
" of Lauderdale, was wedded to Sir Lionel Talmash, of
" Suffolk, and at her father's death she assumed the title of
" Dysart.

" She was a woman of beauty and vast abilities. Her
" quickness of apprehension, and her vivacity of wit, were
" prodigious ; and to these gifts of nature she added a fund
" of literature which, even in this age of *learned ladies*,
" would be esteemed uncommon ; for she not only under-
" stood divinity, history, and philosophy, but even mathe-
" matics. With all these advantages, she was totally devoid
" of principle, and so outrageously covetous, that her hunger
" of riches could never be satiated. During the life of her
" first husband she was intimate with Lauderdale, and sub-
" sequently persuaded him that she had saved his life after
" Worcester fight, through her influence with Cromwell,
" who also was her admirer, and, if report erred not, had
" little reason to complain of her cruelty."   " After the
" Restoration, Lady Dysart imagined that Lauderdale did
" not appear sufficiently grateful, and a suspension of all
" intercourse took place during some years. But her hus-
" band's death reconciled them, and their intimacy became
" so scandalous, that Lauderdale's wife, a daughter of Lord
" Home, could no longer endure the indignity, but retired
" to Paris, where she died, leaving one daughter, afterwards
" married to the Earl of Tweeddale."   " Lady Dysart, in
" process of time, persuaded her old admirer to make her an
" honest woman, and gained so complete an ascendancy,
" that she contrived to incite him to quarrel with his oldest
" and best friends,—among the rest, with Sir Robert Mur-
" ray (whom her father had fixed upon as a husband for
" her), by pretending that he every where gave himself the
" credit of governing Lauderdale. When the Earl achieved

" the supreme command of Scotland, she came down to that
" astonished country in great pomp, and conducted herself
" with such overweening insolence, that she might have
" been mistaken for hereditary princess of the three king-
" doms, instead of grand-daughter to the low-born minister
" of Dysart. She talked with unbounded license of every
" body, set up all places in the Scottish Government to sale,
" with as little shame as cheapness, and levied contribu-
" tions wherever she went. She, in great wrath, even pub-
" licly threatened the Magistrates of Edinburgh for not
" giving her a present, notwithstanding of all the good *she*
" *said* that she had done to them;—though her favours
" were not very obvious, and the Town Council had dis-
" posed of about £17,000 sterling between her husband
" and his creatures. Of two daughters whom she had by
" her first marriage (Kirkton says), she thought she might
" make a better market in Scotland than in England. One
" she married to Argyle's heir (which was a most unhappy
" marriage), and another to the Earl of Murray." The whole
tenor of her conduct has no parallel in Scottish history.

" On 24th August 1682, died, near Tunbridge Wells,
" John Duke of Lauderdale, who, during a great part of
" his sway over Scotland, was almost an absolute monarch
" there. His declining credit at court, and his prodigious
" bulk, were thought to have hastened his death.

" Sir George Mackenzie of Tarbet, writing to the Duke
" of Queensberry from Windsor, on 26th August 1682,
" says, ' The Duchess of Lauderdale hath crowned her
" ' kindness to her late lord by urging him to drink the
" ' waters, which all foretold would kill him, and so it hath
" ' fallen out accordingly.'

" The Duchess took care to secure so much of her estates
" and other property to herself, that his brother (Charles
" Maitland, Lord Hatton), who was his male heir, had

" little to boast of in the richness of his succession. Hatton
" went to law with Her Grace concerning her legacies, and
" for a long time the heads of the law lords were distracted
" with their litigation.

" After she had contrived to make the Duke settle every
" thing he could upon herself and her son by Sir Lionell Tol-
" mache, she was accused of using him most cruelly during
" a disorder brought on by old age, chagrin, and extreme
" corpulence. She died June 1696, and was buried at
" Petersham.

" One of the lampoons composed on the Duchess, to ex-
" pose her character, alludes thus to her intrigues :—

> " ' Methinks this poor land hath been troubled too long
> " ' With Hatton, and Dysart, and old Lidington ;
> " ' While justice provokes me in rhyme to express
> " ' The truth which I know of my bonnie old Bess.
> " ' She is Bess of my heart ; she was Bess of Old Noll ;
> " ' She was once Fleetwood's Bess, and she's now of Athole ;
> " ' She's Bessie of Church, and Bessie of State,' " &c.*

From one of the extracts given in the Appendix, it would
appear that Sir Patrick Home of Lumsdain had been employed professionally, as an advocate, by the Duke of
Lauderdale, and that after his death he took part against
his brother the Earl,—at the instance most probably of the
Duchess, his widow. Perhaps it was at Sir Patrick's sug-
gestion that the Duke had acquired the right of being
titular of the teinds of the parish of Coldingham.

It will have been observed, that the consideration for
which the Duchess disponed to Sir Patrick her house and
lands of Bruntstane, was his " services."

It appears that, after her death, Lord Dysart, her son,

---

* For some farther notices of the Duchess and her doings, see Appendix (E), consisting of extracts from the Diary of Lord Fountainhall,
one of the Judges of the Court of Session.

refused to acknowledge his mother's settlement in favour of
Sir Patrick, and attempted to reside at Bruntstane in spite
of it. In Lord Fountainhall's Decisions, there is a report
of an action of removing against Lord Dysart, at the instance
of Sir Patrick, to compel him to quit the premises.

It is unknown in what way this portrait of the Duchess
came into the possession of the Coldingham Homes ; but it
is most probable that it had been given to Sir Patrick
Home, by the Duke or the Duchess.

Mrs Paterson, before referred to, remembers this picture
well at the house of Burnhall. She states that it hung above
the first landing of the staircase, having on one side of it a
painting of Venus, and on the other side a painting or draw-
ing of a Cupid. These supporters were not inappropriate.

An exact copy of this portrait is in the collection of Lord
Breadalbane, at Taymouth. It also has the repute of being
a Sir P. Lely. The picture had been till lately always at
Holyrood.

IX. Half-length Portrait of an old gentleman, in black
clothes.

This is a portrait of DAVID MILNE, ESQ. OF CAMPIE, near
Edinburgh. His father had been a merchant in Dalkeith.
He himself was a merchant in Edinburgh, and realised a
considerable fortune in business.

The picture was taken when Mr Milne was above eighty
years old. He died in 1816.

It was done by Raeburn, and is considered to be one of
the best paintings he ever executed.

X. Half-length Portrait of a lady, representing GRACE
PURVES, eldest daughter of Sir Alexander Purves of Purves
Hall, by Mary, daughter of Sir James Home of Coldingham.

She died in the year 1814, aged thirty-eight, at Bordeaux, to which place she had gone for her health.

She was married in 1804 to Captain, afterwards Admiral Sir David Milne of Milne-Graden.

XI. Half-length of SIR DAVID MILNE OF MILNE-GRADEN, G.C.B., in his dress as a Rear-Admiral.

The picture is by Raeburn, and is supposed to have been copied by him from a full-length picture, also by Raeburn, which is now at Paxton House.

APPENDIX.

(A), referred to in page 19 of Memoranda.

Mr Johnston of Hilton had four daughters,—viz., Grace, married to Sir James Home of Coldingham ; Sophia, who died unmarried ; married to   Baird of Newbyth, East Lothian; and   married to   St Clair of Longformacus, in Berwickshire.

The family of *Grace*, the eldest, is noticed in the previous part of these Memoranda.

Sophia was known in the family as Aunt Suff. She appears to have resided generally with her niece, Mrs Wauchope of Niddrie. Lord Cockburn, in the Memorials of his Time, speaks thus of her :—" There " was an original ! Her father, from some whim, resolved to see how it " would turn out, and gave her no education whatever. Possessed of " great natural vigour of mind, she passed her youth in utter rusticity ; " in the course of which, however, she made herself a good carpenter " and a good smith, arts which she practised occasionally—even to the " shoeing of a horse, I believe—till after the middle of life. It was not " till after she became a woman, that she taught herself to read and " write ; and then she read incessantly. She must have been about sixty " before I ever saw her, which was chiefly, and often, at Niddrie. Her dress " was always the same,—a man's hat when out of doors, and generally, " when within them, a cloth covering exactly like a man's great-coat, " buttoned closely from the chin to the ground, worsted stockings, " strong shoes, with large brass clasps. In this raiment, she sat in any " drawing-room, and at any table, amidst all the aristocracy of the land, " respected and liked. For her dispositions were excellent, her talk in- " telligent and racy, rich both in old anecdote and in shrewd modern obser- " vation, and spiced with a good deal of plain sarcasm; her understanding " powerful ; all her opinions free, and very freely expressed ; and neither " loneliness nor very slender means ever brought sourness or melancholy " to her face or heart."

Mrs Baird of Newbyth had six sons and five daughters. The daughters were Mrs Wauchope of Niddrie ; Mrs Williamson, afterwards Mrs Swift, who had no issue ; Mrs Rennie, who had several daughters, all unmarried ; Mrs Erskine of Dun ; and Mrs Gordon of Hallhead.

Mrs Wauchope of Niddrie had five sons and five daughters. The daughters were Mrs Mackenzie of Muirton, Mrs Spottiswoode of Spottiswoode, Lady Campbell, Mrs David Wauchope, and Jean, unmarried.

Mrs Erskine of Dun had two daughters, Elizabeth, who died unmarried, and Lady Cassills.

Mrs Gordon of Hallhead had one son, who married Miss Gilmour of the Inch, and one daughter, who married Mr Hope Johnstone of Rachills.

(B), referred to in page 26 of Memoranda.

Presbrie Att Dundee, 29 *Septr*. 1697.

The Presbrie do hereby testify That their Reverend Brother, Mr Ninian Hoome, Minr. at Preston, hath in great diligence and faithfullness served in the Work of the Gospel in our bounds of Angus and Mernes, supplying vacand congregations for the space of fourtteen Sabbaths, wherein his Ministrie was verie savourie and edifying, as well as his conversation amongst us was pious and examplary. As also that he did carefully obey all the appointments of the Presbrie, And by his wise and judicious conduct and peaceable frame of spirit, was singularly vcefull and assistant to us in the exercise of discipline and goverment. So that we humbly tender our hearty thanks to the Reverend Synod of Merse and Teviotdale for sending so well qualified ane helper to us, And to him for coming over to help us in our great desolations. In testimony of the premisses, this, att the Appoyntment of the Presbrie, is Subscribed By

(Signed)   JO: SPALDING, Modr.

This do to testifi to al Concerned, that the Bearer hyeirof, Mr Ninian Hume, Schoolmaster & Precentor at ffogo, hath served wi us thes two zeirs bypast, & ane halfe or thereby, and behaved Himselfe Piously & Christianly, & now Being going on in his Tryals in order to the mistr, we know nothing that may hinder the saminc.—Given at our Session of Fogo the 9 day of May javjt & Nintie six, & subscribed as folows,

(Signed)   P. MOOD, Minir.

(C), referred to in page 27 of Memoranda.

These are all the children mentioned in the pedigree of the family given in the Marchmont Peerage case. But it would rather appear that there must have been more sons and daughters. There is extant a correspondence between Ninian Home of Billie and Lady Wedderburn, from 1718 to 1721, in which reference is made to Johnie, Frankie, George, and Tibie, all apparently residing at Wedderburn, as members of the family.

It is evident from this correspondence that Ninian exerted himself to get the sons out into professions, recommending them to his friends, and supplying them with money. John he sent to London, where he obtained for him employment in the merchant service, and ultimately in a king's ship. Frank became an apprentice to a surgeon, apparently somewhere in Berwickshire. George exceedingly displeased Ninian, and also his mother, in consequence of an attachment he had formed to a Mrs Jamieson, maid to the Countess of Home. In his letter of 15th December 1720, he says,—" I look upon George as lost; give my service to Johnie " and Ffrankie, and my humble respects to Mrs Home and Tibie." " I " cannot express the concern I have upon the account of George his folly, " nor can I give your Lap's any advice how to behave towards him. I " almost think he will not trouble Wedderburn much after this. In re- " gard to his going to the Hirsel and staying there so long, is such a con- " tradiction to your commands, and so contrary to all our opinions, that " I apprehend he is determined to neglect us all and depend upon my " Lady Home, and his new friends, such as they are. Only if he come " back, if your Lap. could bring yourself to take no notice of his crime " in going ther, perhaps it may disappoint ye gentleman, who, I fear, " is seeking an occasion to break with us all, and to cast the blame of his " conduct upon you and some oyrs; for if you take notice of it, so as " to expostulate with him for his breach of your commands, I fear you " will have reason to carry your resentment too far."

Perhaps the George here referred to was Ninian's son by his first wife.

(D), referred to in page 27 of Memoranda.

LETTER, Mr NINIAN HOME to Lady WEDDERBURN.—*Edinboro*, 12th *January* 1721.

MADAM,—I am much satisfied to know yt the nearer poor Johnie is to go away, the fonder he is of going. I have wryt to him ye enclosed short line with no little uneasiness. If he consider it, it will be of some use to him, tho not so distinct and full as it would have been had I been easie at the tyme, and I will say it refreshes me to hear yt ye Doctor has spirit and resolution to push his fortune, and embarks with gladness occasiones yt may enable to do it, and inclines not to loyter about the doors or near at home as George does, whom nothing will satisfie but Mrs Jamison for a wife, and James Hunter for a master, proofs sufficient of no great spirit and lowring mind. I have a letter from him by the earier, but he mistakes me and his measures. It's not a poor whinning letter yt will set him right in my opinion. Again I resolve to give him ane answer by his aunt with the first occasion after this.

If your broy'r be not disposed to make you uneasie, he will certainly send out your seasin and contract, ffor, after what you have wryt, he can have no shadow of excuse for delaying it, and I cannot think but he will also, in answer to yours, declare himself as to what assistance he resolves to give for repairing the house. I cannot trouble your Lap's with ane long account of the state of my health, for its most uncertain. Easter end of ye last week, and untill yesterday morning, I was pretty easie, when the symptoms returned, and last night and this day I am much worse. Every day for some weeks past I take some tincture, emulsion, balsam, or oy'r drug, twice at least a day, and sometymes oftener. But I find little or no relief. I was become verry thin, and every day my flesh sensibly wasted in spite of all the gellies, syrups, and oy'r cordials I got with oysters every morning. But for thes two or three days past every body observes I am no thinner, but rather better. My colour is extream good, and I am never very uneasie but qn I wryt, which increases yt slight pain in my breast and left side. My cough is not worse, and my night sweatings are much abated. I must still trouble you to excuse me to Mrs Home, for, in earnest, I am not able to wryt to her at present. You may believe it is most pleasant to me to hear from you, and qn Wednesday comes I have three or four tymes at the earier befor he comes in. I be ever continued with a true respect, your most obedient servant,

(Signed)   NIN. HOME.

LETTER of ADVICE, Mr NINIAN HOME to JOHN HOME, upon his going abroad.—*Edinburgh, 12th January* 1721.

Digito compesie Libellum.

JOHN,—You are now going abroad, and I think I need not tell you that your eternal happiness and present weelfare depends upon the right conduct and management of yoursel ; and in order to that, above all fear and love God, and let this be expressed in a dayly sincere and serious worshipping and adoring of him as your Creator and Preserver. Be frequent in reading the Scriptures with attention and devotion, and often meditate and think upon what you read. Ever remember that you are in the sight and under the inspection of ane all-seeing God, who is to be your Judge at last, and every night reflect upon and examine all you have done that day; and gein you have failled of your duty, or dishonoured God, intreat his forgiveness of it, and firmly resolve and watch against these failings and sins in tyme coming.

Let it be your care not to disoblige any person, never to speak ill of any person, but endeavour to bear with the faults of oy'rs. To esteem those that deserve it, and pay a civill respect to all you converse with.

In the meanest condition you can fall into, remember you are a gentleman, and of whom you are coume. But never speak of yt to oy'rs, far less boast of it ; but let your actions and behaviour discover it.

You want a ffortune: endeavour not only to gain one, but to deserve it ; and ever believe this, for an uncontested truth, that no estate is like that which a man acquires himself, in ane honest employment, by his diligence, frugality, and care.

Be always observing what makes other men esteemed, and imitate that; and what makes you disesteemed, and avoid yt ; and thus you will dayly grow wiser by marking the conduct and carriage of those you live and converse with.

Be discreet and civill to all you converse with, but intimate and familiar with none but persons of the best sense and greatest virtue you can find : mind that a man among children is long a child, and a child among men soon a man, as the proverb is.

Study honesty and probity. Disdain to lye. Keep your promises, and let your word be sacred, for truth is allowed the most esteemable quality, falsehood and lieng the greatest reproach ; yrfor let honour and honesty govern all your actions. In so doing you will be esteemed by and acceptable to all.

Avoid sudden and rash quarrells as childish and brutal things, and at the same tyme faill not in a civil and respectfull maner, to let everybody know you are not to be ill used.

Accustom yourself to observe men and their actions ; consider and think upon them, and out of these form to yourself rules of conduct and behaviour. It is not the having many preceipts, but the conforming ourselves to a few material ones, yt is our advantage, and yrfor I shall trouble you with no more ; only let me mind you of the state and condition of your family, and that you have had as good education for your business as this nation affords, and a longer tyme allowed you for learning it here than most have ; which I mention, because, with the little thing given you now, is all you are to expect; yrfor govern yourself accordingly, and often reflect upon it, and entertain no thought of having any fortune but what you can make to yourself by your industry, care, and frugality, through the assistance and blessing of God. To whose holy care and safe protection I sincerly commend and commit you; and am, with much truth,

Your affect. true friend and servant,

(Signed)   NIN. HOME.

Copy LETTER, backed " Lady BILLIE to GEORGE HOME, Esq., Ensign " in the Honourable Colonall Sowles' Regement, in Garison at Ghent, " fflanders."

DEIAR GEORDIE,—I just now recived yours, which gave me no small reliefe, it being what I was most impationt for to have hard from you for some time. I presume befor thes you have recived to your gratt affliction the meloncolly acounts of my deiar jual your father's death, whom it pelised the Almightiy God to call for upon the seventeenth of Desmber last. D. Geordie, Its in vaen to imadgen words cane express our loss, the tenderast husband and most lovind and affctnott father was ever in being. You may believe its not eysic for me to writt upon thes subjak without being in the depest meloncolly and affliction; yett as you desir it, I cannot forbeiar to sattesfie you in some mesur as to your deiar father desstemper, which was much as follows:—After being for three munths in the country, he returned upon the 21 of Novmber, till apperance in hes ordnary helth, but was sized the very same night with an sever ashma, which continowed without the smalest respitt, yea, without slip, for twelve days and night, in spitt of all assistance or remeadies used, and yett, notwithstanding of his lod and desstress, which is past expreshan, and sencabell of his approtching death from the ferst moment he was sized, it was surprising how winderfully he was suported, and with what resollution, coureige, and firmness he bore up to the last, and, att the same time, with the gratest resegnation to the devine will of God. After the 12 day of hiss illness the ashma abeted some what, but he becam to be shure much waker, but till appiarance relay cysir, which gave no smal confort;—in which time, tilll it peliased God to remouve hem, he dcrected anent all hes affaers, yea, to the smalst poynt, even his oun faunarls, with so much calmness and composour of mind. He was sencabell to the last, and I am convinced imbraced his chiang with chiarfullness; and as my deiar juall has been peliased to repos such confiedence in me as to intrust me with all your conserns, be ashured, with the assistance of God, all shall be safe and fathfully taken care of till it pelias God you return, which I both hop for and expacts so soon as convenant for you. I proposed to have writt to you long or thes, but was persudad from it, ashuring me it oud not find you ther ; but if you receive this, I beg youll lett me hier from you, which I ashure you will always give pelisur and satasfaction to

Dear Geordie,*

Your affetnott mother,

MARGARET HOME.

Ednbrugh, 19 *Januarie* 1745.

The childriug offors all ther love, and desirs to be remembred to you, and heartly wishes to see you.

*Copy of ye advice sent to Geordie
by his Father, holograph of Mr
Home, to be writ over by me as
soon as possible as the Copy is,
and its torn.*

MEMORANDUM of ADVICES sent to GEORDIE.

Your concerns are of more account with me than my own ; and I send you no compliment when I assure you that I will make this appear in ye manner you desire. I take ane intcrest in whatever concerns you, and without yt assurance you ought to be persuaded of it. I have all the sentiments of gratitude I ought to have, and will not faill, qrever I have opportunity, to give you proofs of my real sense of it.

Remove the impressions you may have received to my disadvantage. When I devoted myself to your interests, I did it without reserve, and with a settled resolution of our continuing in the same dependance and steady resignation to your will.

I persuade myself that my perfect fidelity to your interests will oblige you to acknowledge it to be yours, etc. What was an additional mortification seemed to be fallen from yt share in your favour, which you had done me the honour to promise me.

I am guilty of no oy'r crime but yt of having been devoted to, etc. ; and it shall be my constant care to preserve, etc., in all my future conduct.

1. In the first place, mind your duty to God ; ffear and love him above

---

* There is among the Paxton Papers a Commission, signed by General George Wade, Field Marshall of His Majesty's Forces in Flanders, in favour of George Home, gentleman, appointing him Ensign of that Company of Foot whereof Colonel Robinson Sowles is Captain, dated at Berlegham, 21st June 1744.

D

all, and endeavour to manifest your love and ffear of him by ane universal respect and obedience to his laws; and, with all the ffirmness and resolution possible, resolve against that detestable custom, swearing.

2. Abhore lying and dissimulation, and everything you know is false.

3. Avoid all wrangling and contradiction. In conversation, tell yor sentiments of things which fall in discourse wt modesty, and a deference to the judgement of ory'rs, even when you cannot intirely agree with ym in opinion, bearing in mind always yt it is equally probable you may be mistaken as well as ym.

4. Refrain from all personal quarrels, and the giving of offence to any body; and never utter ane indecent word, even to your inferiors.

5. Observe sobriety and temperance both in eating and drinking, ffor nothing unmans one more; therefore shunn it as you wish to preserve the health and vigour of both body and mind, and receive the favour and good opinion of all worthy and thinking men.

6. Be exact and punctual in performing what you promise, and never engage your word except you be sure of having it in your power to perform.

7. Be always decent in your dress and clean in your linnen, ffor decencey and cleanliness are commendable and becoming; but all superfluities in apparel discovers rather a softness.

8. If ever you come to be ane officer, and to have the command of oy'rs, avoid all cruelty and barbarous treating of the common soldiers, and endeavour to procure their respect and affection by kindness and humanity, and to recover ym from yr faults and errors by kind reproofs. And if you be so unlucky as to have stubborn and irredeemable dispositions, discharge ym rather than use violence, for it must disturb you, and may infect and corrup oy'rs.

(E), referred to in page 39 of Memoranda.

" *March* 1683.—A process was raised in Exchequer against the Magis-
" trates of Edinburgh by certain merchants. This process was designed
" to expiscat what wrytes had been given to Ministers of State, or the
" Duchesse of Lauderdale or others, which the Treasurer called The mys-
" tery of iniquity."

" *April* 1684.—The High Treasurer and Treasurer-Depute had fre-
" quent meetings on the toune of Edinburgh's count and reckoning."
" They refused to allow the article of £6000 payed to the Duke and
" Duchesse of Lauderdale."

" *Sept.* 1684.—Mr Carstairs is brought before the Secret Committee
" of Counsell, and is tortured with the thumbikens, and confessed there
" has bein a current plot in Scotland these ten years past. He named
" many that were upon the knowledge of it, as Murray of Philliphaugh,
" Pringle of Torwoodlee, Home of Polwart, Home of Bassinden, &c. ;
" and some gave out the Dutchesse of Lauderdale as a resetter of Argile
" since his forfaulter, and a furnisher of him with money."

" *December* 1684.—The Duchesse of Lauderdale's affair against the
" Earle of Lauderdale was advised. The Earle and the Lord Mait-
" land, his son, in the Duke's lifetyme, signed a ratification of the
" rights of Leidington, Dudiston, &c., disponed by him to his Dutchesse,
" they being charged on this ratification, suspend, that it was a con-
" ditional oblishment." "My Lord Lauderdale gave in a declinator
" against Harcous (one of the Judges), upon this ground, that he had
" formed and drawen the wholle securities and writs granted by the
" Duke to his Dutchesse, and so had given partiall counsell, and wld
" judge himself concerned to maintain his oune deeds. He desired
" these of the Lords that had not done the like, to throw the first stone
" at him." "The Lords sustained not the declinator, but allowed him
" to sit and vote with them, in regard he deponed he was intrusted
" and employed by both parties to draw these writs." "Pitmedden argued
" that such donations to wives ought not to be encouraged, for that
" exposed old men to be ther wives' pray."

" 18 *Jan.* 1685.—There is a letter from His Majesty to the Lords of
" Session in favors of the Dutchesse of Lauderdale, against the Earle,
" obtained by Lundie, Secretary, and the Lord Guildford North, Chan-
" celor of England, bearing that he had considered their interlocutor,
" and found it to be douneright contrare to the Earle's oblishment and
" ratification, and commanding them to give ane account of the same,
" and stop any farder procedor till he declare his pleasure." " The
" Lords having considered the King's letter, they appointed the Presi-
" dent, Register, King's Advocate, and Pitmedden, to forme the draft of
" ane apologetick letter to the King, giving him a short hint of the
" grounds of that affair, and representing that his royal predecessors
" had founded that Court with a power to determine finally and ulti-
" mately, without any appeall either to the King or Parliament. How-
" ever, they submitted to His Majestie's royal pleasure in the case."

" *Feb.* 1686.—There is a letter read to the Lords from the King, pro-
" cured by the Lord Maitland (who had got this favor by the Priests for
" changing his religion to serve a turn), against the Dutchesse of Lau-
" derdale, altering his former letter this far, that for the standing of the
" family of Lauderdale, they may submet the affair to some of the Lords,
" who may determine to her a reasonable joynture. This she took in

" very bad part; and the President loves not this way of ruling the
" Session by letters."

" *March* 1688.—The Dutchess of Lauderdale pursues Sir James Dick
" of Priestfield for ane ryot, in so far as shee having taken out of Dud-
" dingston Loch five of the swans, which, or their parents, were put in
" by her Lord, he took them back again, except two, whose skins shee
" had given to General Drummond in his sicknes, to warm his breast,
" alleged the Swans were his own, he standing infeft in the Loch, and
" consequently in all that fed on it.

" The Lords fand, if the Swans had come of their own accord, and
" bigged there, then they were Sir James' ; but since the owner, who put
" them in, was knowen, they fand they belonged to the Duchess, and Sir
" James his tolerance to let them stay in his Loch, did not make them
" his ;" " upon which he turned all the rest out of the Loch."